The Farmer's Three Sons

Chantal de Marolles was born in Lyon, France, in 1940. After studying Russian and Asian languages, she began to write children's stories that have been published by Grasset Jeunesse, Fleurus, Centurion, and Bayard Presse. Married with four children, she lives in a suburb of Paris and spends her spare time painting.

Claude and Denise Millet studied at the Arts Decoratifs in Paris. Since then, they have worked together, doing illustrations for advertisements, newspapers, and publishers. They are published by Hachette, Gallimard, Centurion, and work regularly for Bayard Presse.

Library of Congress Cataloging-in-Publication Data
available upon request
ISBN 0-89565-816-X

The Farmer's Three Sons

A story written by Chantal de Marolles
illustrated by Claude and Denise Millet

THE CHILD'S WORLD
MANKATO, MINNESOTA

When his three sons had grown up, their father, Frank, thought to himself, "Maybe my sons don't want to be farmers like me. They need to find out for themselves what they want to do."

Soon after he called Garry, the oldest,
and said "Garry, listen to me.
You're done with school now.
I'm going to give you a year off to tour
the world and see how you make out."

Garry yelled,
"Hooray!
A year off, how wonderful,
I'll leave right away!"

His mother told him,
"Wait, I've made you two sturdy bags of
good cloth. In one I put a vest, a shirt,
and some socks and in the other, a large
loaf of bread, some cheese, and jam. In
one year, when you come back, try to
bring back the two sacks because I
worked very hard on them."

Garry exclaimed,
"Yes, yes, good-bye Mom and Dad
and my two brothers!"

And he headed out right away,
one bag on his right shoulder,
the other on his left.
Never had Garry felt so happy.
It seemed to him that the wheat was
yellower, the grass greener,
and the sky bluer
than it had ever been.
But at the end of two days,
he had eaten all his food.
Garry was hungry.
Then he said to himself,
 "Hum, it's hot and it's almost summer.
I'll sell my vest to buy some cakes."

For two weeks,
Garry ate cream puffs.
Then he sold his shirt,
his socks, and his bags.
When he had sold everything,
he decided to work,
but not on a farm
or in a field, oh no!
that was much too hard.
Garry went to the inns*
and he sang at the top of
his lungs to distract* the customers.

* These words are explained on page 45, numbers 1 and 2.

Because he sang well
and he was a nice guy,
he was invited to all the weddings
and all the parties.
Garry was having such a good time
that he didn't notice time passing.
One day, however, Garry noticed
that his shirt was as full
of holes as a piece of lace
and all that was left of his socks
were a few threads.
Then Garry said to himself,
"It's time to go back home,
besides, it's been about a year
that I've been gone."

When he was near the farm,
his mother ran out to meet him,
"Garry, my poor boy,
what a raggedy man* you are!
And someone stole
your sturdy bags!"

Garry bursts out laughing,
"No, Mom,
see, I sold them.

* This word is explained on page 46, number 3.

If you only knew what
a good time I had!
Everywhere I went people
asked me to sing for them.
Listen! I wrote a song,
I'll sing it for you."

But his father grumbled,
"You can sing later,
right now we have to make hay."

That night in bed,
Frank said to his wife,
"Our Garry is certainly
a good singer,
he doesn't want to be a farmer.
Tomorrow,
I'll let Greg go for a year to tour the
world. Then we'll see what happens."

When his mother gave Greg his two bags,
he looked them over and said,
"They're smaller than the ones
you made for Garry,
you should make me a third one."

His mother sighed a little,
but she made him a third bag.
Greg was astonished,
"But this bag is empty!"
"Oh, Greg!" his mother said,
"You always want more than the others.
All right, here are some nuts."

Greg headed out right away,
one bag on his left shoulder,
the other on his right and
the third hanging around his neck.

Before entering a town,
Greg would pick bouquets of flowers
and kill thrushes* with
his sling-shot.
Then he sold them and he bought
a fourth bag to carry his money.

* This word is explained on page 46, number 4.

After ten days on the road,
Greg bought a wheelbarrow
to help him carry
all his new bags filled to
the brim with thrushes,
fabric, cakes, toys, and tools.
As soon as he got to a town,
all the women would come running up,
"Do you have a thimble? A book?
Some forks? A broom?"

Oh yes, of course, Greg had it all!

He kept everything
in his twenty-five bags
piled up in his cart*
and in the two other bags
that his donkey carried.
Greg was so busy that he
didn't notice the time passing.
At the end of a year,
without really knowing how,
he came to his parents' farm.

* This word is explained on page 47, number 5.

His mother yelled,
"Here is our Greg!
Frank, our son has come back!
And look at all those bags,
surely he has the shovel
that you need."

Greg said, "Sure I do.
Here it is and that will be six dollars."

His father Frank grumbled,
"Six dollars? That's just about how
much your dinner will cost you tonight.
But first come and help me
milk* the cows."

* This word is explained on page 47, number 6.

That night in bed,
Frank said to his wife,
"Our Greg is a good merchant,
and I'd be surprised if he
wanted to be a farmer.
Tomorrow,
George will leave to tour the world
and then we'll see."

And the next day, George headed out,
one bag on his left shoulder,
the other on his right.
It was a nice day and
George whistled while he walked.
Soon he met a farmer who told him,
"You're lucky, my boy,
to have the time to go for a walk.
Me, I don't even have time to eat lunch
because I still have a field to plow."

George said,
"I have enough in my bag
for two to eat,
we can split it,
and then I'll help you.
That way I'll learn how to do it."

When they were finished,
the farmer brought George home
and filled his empty bag
with bread and ham.

George headed out again and toward
evening he heard a cry for help.
It was an old peasant
who had slipped into a pit.
George immediately helped
him get out and offered him
the clothes that he had
in his second bag, telling him,
"You need to change clothes,
otherwise you'll catch cold."

When the peasant had changed clothes,
he told George,
"If I get sick, it's no big deal, because I
know how to cure myself with herbs.
If you want, I can teach you to
recognize them and pick them,
and we can fill up your bag."

All George's days
passed like that,
he gave and he received,
so he always had an empty bag
and a full one.

40

He learned so many things
that the year passed quickly.
And, of course, when he went home,
he had a bag full of presents
for everyone.

Then Frank says to his wife,
"Ah, wife of mine! How lucky
we are to have three such sons -
Garry never has anything
in his hands or his pockets,
but his heart is full of songs
and he will be a great singer.
Greg is always very busy,
he's not lazy and
he will be a good merchant.
And now George, watch him,
he is like a well-tended field,
ready to receive and ready to give, and
that means he will be a true farmer!"

WORDS FROM THE STORY

1. **An inn** is a house
where you can sleep
and eat like in a hotel.

2. **Distracting** means to get the
attention of someone who's
trying to do something else.
If they are working, it is annoying,
but if they're bored, it's amusing.

3. Rags are old torn-up clothes.
Raggedy men wear them.

4. **The thrush** is a bird
from the blackbird family.
They have brown wings and a white
stomach speckled with black spots.

5. **A cart** is a small wagon that can be covered with a roof.

6. **To milk** a cow, you pull on its udder. You can milk by hand or with a machine.